Harley's Gift

HARLEY'S GIFT

by

Beth Pollock

To Kathryn,

Enjoy!

Beth Pollock

James Lorimer & Company Ltd., Publishers
Toronto

James Lorimer & Company Ltd. acknowledges the support of the Ontario Arts Council. We acknowledge the support of the Government of Canada through the Book Publishing Industry Development Program (BPIDP) for our publishing activities. We acknowledge the support of the Canada Council for the Arts for our publishing program. We acknowledge the support of the Government of Ontario through the Ontario Media Development Corporation's Ontario Book Initiative.

Cover design: Kate Moore

The Canada Council | Le Conseil des Arts
for the Arts | du Canada

ONTARIO ARTS COUNCIL
CONSEIL DES ARTS DE L'ONTARIO

Library and Archives Canada Cataloguing in Publication

Pollock, Beth
    Harley's gift / Beth Pollock.
(Streetlights)

ISBN 978-1-55028-992-3
    1. Family--Juvenile fiction. 2. Christmas--Juvenile fiction.
I. Title. II. Series.
PS8631.O45H37 2007   jC813'.6   C2007-905910-4

James Lorimer & Company Ltd.,
Publishers
317 Adelaide Street West
Suite 1002
Toronto, Ontario, M5V 1P9
www.lorimer.ca
Printed and bound in Canada.

Distributed in the
United States by:
Orca Book Publishers
P.O. Box 468
Custer, WA USA
98240-0468

To Andrew, Emily and Rachel,
for believing in me.

1

"If you could get anything you wanted for Christmas, what would it be?" I asked.

My mom answered the way parents always do. "Whatever you give me will be awesome."

Christmas was just over a week away. We had finished our Saturday grocery shopping, and the song "We Three Kings" was playing as we walked out the door of No Frills.

"Okay, but if you could pick anything in the world, what would you ask for?"

Mom tugged on her blonde ponytail, thinking. "I'd love a big backyard with a garden. But then I'd need time to work in it, right?" She shrugged. "What about you, Harley?"

"Someone to carry our groceries home."

Actually, my number-one wish was for Mom and Grandma to be friends. For the last eleven years — and maybe before I was born, too — they hadn't got along with each other. They didn't usually fight, but they didn't hug or call each other either. When they did talk on the phone, it was only to arrange one of my visits.

Someone to carry our groceries home was a good second-place wish, though. Shopping for food was heavy work. At least we had a couple of bundle buggies, so we could push the groceries home instead of carrying them. The wheels squeaked, but without bundle buggies we'd be going to No Frills three times a week.

The worst part was the bright yellow bags with *No Frills* stamped in black. Why couldn't they use white plastic bags like every other store? When we walked home, everybody knew where we'd been shopping. Even worse was carrying the empty yellow bags to the store, so we wouldn't have to pay for new ones.

"Hey, where are your gloves?" Mom asked.

Mom had told me to put on gloves before we left home. I hadn't bothered because they're ugly. But now my hands were freezing, and I wished I'd worn them.

We were waiting for the light to change at the corner when I heard a commotion across the street. A lady was yelling at Prince Charlie.

"Don't take up so much of the sidewalk!"

Charlie didn't pay any attention. He held his baseball cap in the other direction and jingled the coins.

The light changed and Mom began to cross.

"Mom," I said, grabbing her arm. "Can we wait 'til she's gone?" I pointed to the lady. I could hardly make out what she was saying, but she was jabbing the air with her finger. Charlie was still seated, looking up at her.

"It's too cold to stand here. We'll be past them in a sec."

I paused.

"C'mon, Harley. I don't want to miss the light," she said, and kept crossing.

By the time I decided to follow her, Mom was

half a block ahead. I got to the other sidewalk just as cars started pouring through the intersection.

Now I was close enough to hear the whole conversation.

"You're blocking the sidewalk. This is a public place!"

"You think you can get out of your car, shout at me, and drive back home," said Charlie. "But you don't even know me."

I looked at the lady more closely. She was holding the passenger door of a big shiny car open a bit. Charlie was sitting right where the door would be if it was open all the way. The lady was wearing a soft brown coat with a furry collar. Her smooth leather gloves matched her boots.

Then I looked at Charlie. The only warm thing about him was the cigarette dangling from his mouth. He wore a thin beige jacket, the kind you'd wear in May, not in the middle of a Toronto winter. His hands were stuffed in his jeans pockets as far as they'd go and his shoulders were hunched forward. He had collected five or six coins in the bottom of his Blue Jays cap.

"Must be nice sitting around all day begging money for cigarettes?" the lady said.

Charlie wasn't a bad guy. He never hurt anyone. He sat on the street corner and held out his hat for money. Sometimes when it was warm outside, he sang too.

"Harley!"

All three of us looked up. Mom had finally realized I was way behind her. I reached in my pocket. All I had was a couple of dimes. I jingled them for a second and thought about giving one to Charlie, but I didn't want to get in the middle of the fight. I looked away and ran to catch up to Mom.

She pushed in her buggy next to the dollar store, so she wouldn't block the sidewalk. "What was happening there?" she asked.

"Nothing," I said. I didn't want to talk about it. Maybe I should have stood up for Charlie, or at least given him some money.

"Okay, then let's get home. The milk is going to freeze."

I didn't know if the milk would freeze, but I

knew *I* would if we didn't get home soon. I squeezed my hands into fists to warm them up, and curled my toes inside my boots to keep them from going numb.

We walked another block, then turned right onto our street. We walked by my best friend Naomi's house, but I knew no one was home. Naomi's family had strung Christmas lights on the front shrubs, and they also had a menorah in the front window. For a family who never went to church, they believed in covering all the bases.

"I forgot to tell you," Mom said. "Naomi's mom called. She wanted to know if we were free to come for brunch on Boxing Day. I told her we'd be there."

I pumped my arm. "Yes!"

Naomi's house was the opposite of ours, in every way. Our house was always tidy — except my room. Mom thought knick-knacks were dust collectors, so she didn't have many sitting out. And at dinner, Mom and I took turns talking about our day.

Nobody at Naomi's house took turns. Sometimes they had debates at the kitchen table; sometimes they recited lines from plays I hadn't heard of. Naomi's mom had a collection of 184 pairs of salt and pepper shakers. I'd been to their place a lot, and I hadn't used the same salt shaker twice. The last time I was over, we made papier-mâché cats on the living-room floor. I could never live at Naomi's house, but I loved to visit.

"And your dad called."

I rolled my eyes.

"He wants to see you before Christmas."

Good old Frank. Every year, he came to Toronto the week before Christmas to bring me a present and tell Mom she hasn't changed since high school. Of course she'd changed. She had a baby before she graduated — me.

"If I have to," I said.

"I said he could swing by tomorrow afternoon."

I didn't say anything. It wasn't my idea of a good time, but at least I'd get it over with for another year.

"I know you hate seeing him," she said. "It's

no fun for me, either. But I really want us to try to get along."

"Why? It's not as if we like him or anything."

"I want him to see how amazing you turned out. And to see that we're doing okay, you know? That he doesn't have to pity us."

So that's why Mom cleaned even more obsessively before he came, and why I had to wear my best clothes. "I'll be good," I said. But I wished Mom would get together with Grandma at Christmas instead.

When we got home, I lugged some bags onto the front porch and stamped the snow off my boots. Inside, I put the bags on the counter and took my coat off. I had to be careful because my zipper was broken. When I unzipped too quickly, the little pull-thing came off the track and Mom had to fix it.

As soon as she went out to get the rest of the food, I grabbed the bag of Oreos. I had just taken a bite of one when Mom called, "Hey, can you give me a hand here?"

"Mmm-hmm," I said, swallowing the evidence.

I ran to the front door and reached to help her carry the bags in.

She smiled. "How was the Oreo?"

I'd never be a good criminal.

Mom laughed as we carried the grocery bags into the kitchen. "Save the rest for dessert, okay?" She opened the bag with the meat. "Sausages tonight?"

"Sure." I didn't like cooking sausages — they splattered grease all over the stove and me. Thank goodness Mom cooked on Saturdays. She'd make them tonight and we'd put the rest in the freezer. We had a lot because they were on sale.

After our cold walk home, I was glad to be in the warm house. Freezing rain splattered on the window. I looked out at the empty hook where Mom put the hummingbird feeder in the spring. She loved watching the birds dip their long beaks in and out of the sugar-water mixture. I thought they were more like electric toothbrushes than birds, all skinny and whirring.

"Good thing we got home before the freezing

rain started falling," she said. "Could you move the mums off the table? And straighten up the living room while you're in there."

I carried the vase into the living room and set it on the side table, sloshing some water as I set it down. We might run short on other things between paydays, but we always had flowers. Mom worked at Ripley's Florists, and she brought home the slightly wilted flowers.

The phone rang and Mom picked it up in the kitchen. I tried wiping up the spill with my T-shirt, but it got soaked through. As I opened the kitchen door to get a cloth, I heard Mom saying, "I don't know what to do. I can't afford — " She looked up and saw me standing in the doorway. She blushed and turned away. "Just a sec, Heather," she mumbled into the phone.

"Harley, the Tide's in the bag by the door," she said, one hand covering the receiver. "Take it down to the washer for me, okay?"

That was weird. Mom talked to Aunt Heather at least twice a week, and their discussions were never private.

I hesitated on the landing, thinking I might hear the rest of the conversation, but Mom peered around the corner until I started down the stairs.

As I carried the bag to the laundry room, I wondered what it was that Mom couldn't afford, and why she looked so upset.

2

"You look great, kiddo."

Mom had French-braided my hair and tied it in a navy ribbon to match my dress. She caught my eye in the mirror, and I felt embarrassed about liking the way I looked. So I curled my lips to bare my teeth and opened my mouth wide. Mom laughed when she saw my goofy face.

I had tried to find out about her phone conversation yesterday, but she had just told me how great Aunt Heather and her family were doing. I wanted to know what it was that we couldn't afford, but the memory of Mom's sad face kept me from asking.

A car screeched to a stop outside our house.

Mom looked out the living room window. "Frank's here," she said.

A man wearing a suede jacket climbed out of a shiny silver car. It was Frank, all right. Typical car salesman — he always drove the latest model. He pulled some presents out of the trunk.

"I guess I have to be nice to him," I said.

"Do your best," said Mom, brushing the bangs away from my eyes.

Frank rang the doorbell. Mom didn't move. Neither did I. "Doing your best would start with answering the door," she said.

I sauntered over and opened it.

"Look at you, baby girl," he said, "I can't believe how much you've grown!"

He said that every year. I was dying to say, "I can't believe how much you've grown, too!" But I didn't think that would fit Mom's definition of being nice.

He grinned at Mom. "Robin, you look great! You never change!"

Mom said, "Hey, Frank."

I couldn't believe she used to like him. And I

really couldn't believe I was related to him. Mom led him into the living room and I followed.

"I brought you a few presents," he said to me. He set three packages on the table. "Don't open the red one! It's a dress, and I can tell it's way too small. I didn't know you'd be so tall."

Duh. Didn't the kids in his other family get taller every year too?

He handed me a small package and I opened it. Three little chapter books. I would have read them when I was six.

"Thank you, sir," I said.

"Who are you calling sir? Don't you remember? I want you to call me Frank!"

"Right." I had remembered. That's why I called him 'sir'. "Thank you, Frank."

He handed me the third gift. "I think you'll like this one."

I opened the card first. It was one of those joke cards with a bug-eyed cat wearing a Santa hat. On the inside it said, *Merry Christmas from Santa Claws*. Trust Frank to find the corniest card ever.

The present was covered in tons of tape. It looked like he had let his kids wrap it. I picked up a pair of scissors and started cutting through the mass of tape and shiny paper. Frank cleared his throat. The furnace clicked on. He jingled some change in his pocket and the floor creaked as he shifted his weight. No one said a word.

As I struggled with the wrapping paper, I saw him glance at his huge silver watch. He'd been in our house less than ten minutes and he was checking the time already? That was a record, even for Frank.

Finally, I tore off the last layer of wrapping paper. Inside was a box of CDs, seven or eight, and most of them were good. One was a CD that Mom would never let me listen to, if she knew. And the new Maddie McDermott CD!

"I hope they're okay," Frank said. "I checked with the kid working at the store and our neighbour's thirteen-year-old daughter."

Mom was standing behind him, shaking her head and putting her finger to her lips. I pretended not to notice. This was probably the best gift he'd ever given me. Except —

"We don't have a CD player," I said.

Frank's face turned red. "I'm sorry. I just assumed …"

He looked so embarrassed, I almost felt sorry for him.

"Ours died a couple of months ago and I haven't got around to buying another one," said Mom. I was sure we just couldn't afford it right now. She came around and stood beside Frank. "Harley's friend Naomi has a CD player. The girls can listen to them at Naomi's place." She raised an eyebrow at me. I knew what *that* meant.

"Thank you," I said. It *was* a good gift, and now that I'd embarrassed Frank, I could be as polite as Mom wanted. I smiled. Frank gave me a thumbs-up.

He grinned at Mom and suddenly I felt a rush of love for her. Frank was the guy who had dumped her when she was pregnant, and left her to raise a baby by herself. He came to see us once a year, driving an expensive car, with gifts that were totally wrong, and Mom went out of her way to make him feel good. Even though I liked seeing him squirm, I wanted to be as nice as she was.

Frank stayed another hour and a half. Mom served tea and cookies. He walked around the block with me and told me to keep my grades up. He showed us a picture of his other kids at Halloween — Ryan dressed as a dinosaur, Amanda in a fairy costume. Mom and I were nice to him the whole time.

"Well," he finally said, "gotta go. It's a four-hour drive, and Sunday's our family dinner night. Sandy and the kids will kill me if I miss it." He reached out to tug on my braid. "Good to see ya. One of these times I'll bring the kids so you can meet them. We should see each other more often."

He said that every year, too.

When Frank left, he honked and waved before speeding away.

"That's it until next year," I said. I lifted the box of CDs and put them under the Christmas tree.

Mom's shoulders relaxed and she let out a breath that she'd probably been holding since Frank had arrived. "That wasn't so bad, was it?" she asked.

"I guess not," I said. I was tired. Sometimes it was hard work being polite.

She put her arm around my shoulder. "I know he's kind of a goof, but he means well."

"Whatever," I said. "I hate it when he pulls out pictures of his real family. They're so perfect."

"You're pretty awesome, yourself," said Mom. "Anyway, they live with him and you don't, so who's the lucky one?" She stood up. "I want to show you something. Come in my bedroom for a sec."

I sat on her bed and Mom reached in the cedar chest. She pulled out a lot of stuff — I saw some sweet little baby clothes that I used to wear — and finally she brought out a photo album.

She sat beside me on the bed and opened the album. I saw a picture of a little girl in a weird striped dress sitting on Santa's lap. "Is that you?" I asked. She looked exactly like I did in kindergarten, except for the dress.

"Like the dress?" Mom asked. She laughed. "I was five that Christmas. Now you know why I never pull out these old pictures." She flipped a few pages and hesitated. She was about to turn the page when I saw a picture and stopped her.

"Mom, were you on the track team?" She was posing with two other girls, and they were all grinning and holding ribbons.

"Yeah, I ruled the 400 metres."

Sometimes when I walked by the high school, I saw the track team training. They wore these blue shorts and yellow T-shirts, and ran by me like gazelles. They seemed like the kind of people who had perfect lives. I couldn't imagine Mom being on the track team.

She turned toward the end of the album. "Here's the one I wanted to show you."

I stared at it. Mom had the same blonde hair as the girl in the picture, the same eyes and nose. But Mom was always so tired. The girl in this picture didn't look tired at all. Her hair was pulled up and she wore a long black dress.

"That's me at the semi-formal in grade eleven,"

said Mom. "And that's Frank."

I looked at the boy standing beside the young Mom. I couldn't believe it. He was actually kind of cute, though a lot skinnier. He had his arm around Mom's shoulders.

I looked up from the album and noticed Mom watching me, waiting for me to say something.

"So, I guess he wasn't always a loser," I said.

"Are you kidding? The guy has a great job, cool car, supports three kids — and he's not even thirty! He's *not* a loser."

I shrugged. "Just because we're related doesn't mean I have to like him." I picked up one of the baby outfits that Mom had put on the bed. It was a little yellow hand-knit dress. I couldn't believe I was ever that small.

She sighed. "Maybe we should talk more about Frank, about the past. You know, I wouldn't want to live with him, even in a mansion. *You're* my family."

She was right. The two of us were happy in our little house.

"But you know," she said, "Frank isn't a bad

guy. He's sent us money every month since you were born."

I knew he gave us money, but I didn't want to think of him as a good guy. "I bet he only does it because some judge makes him."

"I never asked him for a penny. He didn't send much in the early days — he was still in high school. But he always sent something, even though his parents totally ignored me."

I didn't know what to say. I had to get used to the idea of Frank being helpful.

I flipped back to the page that showed Mom with Santa. Beside it was a family picture taken when Mom was about ten. She was standing next to Grandma with her hand on Grandma's shoulder.

"You guys look like you're friends in this picture," I said.

"Must have been a good day."

"Why don't you get along?"

"Your grandmother didn't always approve of the things I did." Mom always called her mother "your grandmother".

That wasn't news to me. I was a little kid when we lived with Grandma, but I still remembered some of their fights. "What didn't she approve of? Was it because of me?"

She shook her head. "Seems like we've been arguing forever. We're just really different people."

Mom and I never talked like this and I wanted to hear more. "I'm eleven now, and I'm old enough to hear the truth. Tell me what happened."

She sat down in the chair beside me and rubbed the back of her neck. "When I found out I was pregnant, it was so bad. It wasn't exactly in her plans for me to have a baby at seventeen. I guess it wasn't in my plans either." She took my hand. "You know I wouldn't change a thing."

I knew that. "But that was ages ago. Why haven't you guys patched things up?"

"It's more than that. Sometimes she tries to solve every problem by throwing money at it. And she'd say the problem is that I'm too stubborn to take her help." Mom laughed. "You know what? We're both right." She glanced at the family picture again. "I can't complain, though. When my dad died, we got a bit of cash that helped me buy a house and move out."

"I can't believe you guys would lose each other over money," I said. "Why don't you both say sorry and start again?"

"Your grandmother and I said things that were hard to take back, and hard to forget."

"Hold on a sec. Why do I have to stay in touch with Frank when you hardly talk to Grandma?"

Mom paused, then laughed. "Got me there, kid." She closed the album and put it back in the cedar chest. "Anyway, enough about that. Let's clean the living room."

There wasn't much cleaning to do. We folded the wrapping paper and ribbon from Frank's gifts and put them aside to use again. Mom set his card on the table beside our Christmas tree.

We had put up the tree and decorated it the weekend before. Mom's favourite ornament was the star I made in kindergarten from the top of a margarine tub. She had been all teary when she put it at the top of the tree, just like she gets every year. I thought we were ready for a new star, but she said she'd use that one forever.

Mom thought the subject of her and Grandma was dropped when she said we should clean, but I wasn't falling for that. She and Grandma were my two favourite people in the world, and it bugged me that they didn't like each other. It would be great if the three of us could spend time together, like a real family.

I thought back to our discussion of the day before. What I wanted for Christmas more than anything was for Grandma and Mom to be friends. But that wasn't the kind of gift I'd find under the tree on Christmas morning.

No, if that's what I really wanted, I'd have to figure out a way to make it happen.

3

"I don't think Mom's giving me a Christmas present this year," I said.

Naomi and I were listening to the Maddie McDermott CD at her place on Tuesday after school. I'd heard three of the songs on the radio, but the rest were new to me.

"Don't be ridiculous," said Naomi. "Of course she'll get you a present."

"Usually she asks me for ideas in November. Next Monday is Christmas and she hasn't said a word about it yet."

"Maybe she'll go shopping at the last minute."

"Mom's way too organized. She doesn't leave anything to the last minute." I'd been thinking

31

about Mom's phone call with Aunt Heather. She didn't spend money on anything that wasn't necessary. I could think of only one thing that she couldn't afford, and that she'd be so upset about — Christmas presents.

"Well, you have to look."

"Look at what?"

"Snoop. Haven't you ever snooped for a present?"

I didn't answer. Naomi gasped. "You've never snooped for a Christmas present? I can't believe it! Now's the time. You gotta rip your house apart until you find it!"

When I got home, I thought about what Naomi had said. Mom had always come through at Christmas, but things had been tight this fall. She'd been cutting her own hair instead of going to the stylist, and she turned the furnace down every time I turned it up. If I told her I was cold she'd say, "Put on a sweater."

Naomi was my best friend, but she didn't know what it was like to think about money all the time. She didn't have to wear second-hand clothes or walk to get her groceries. Most of the time I didn't care about that, but sometimes — like when I didn't know if we could afford Christmas — I wished we weren't so poor. If only Mom wasn't proud, and let Grandma give us money. Listening to CDs at Naomi's house was fun, but I'd love to have a CD player again. And it would be fun to buy new clothes from a really great store.

I put the tuna casserole in the oven. *Don't be silly*, I told myself. *Mom always comes through for me.* But she wouldn't be home for a half-hour and it wouldn't hurt to snoop a little. I knew I wouldn't stop thinking about it until I was sure. Our house was small, so there weren't many hiding places. If there was a present hidden somewhere, I'd find it.

I decided to start in the hall closet. Mom kept all kinds of things in there. Even though I was alone, I tiptoed down the hall and cringed when the closet door creaked open. I reached behind the towels and groped around.

Nothing.

I checked all the shelves in the hall closet,

rummaging behind the extra blankets and under the pillowcases. I even climbed on a chair to peek behind the giant bag of toilet paper at the top.

Nothing.

Where else would she hide a present?

I looked under the oven. A roasting pan, a couple of muffin tins. No gift.

I looked in the drawer beside the fridge. A pair of scissors, a roll of tape, a bunch of pens. No gift.

Maybe she had hidden it somewhere less obvious. I climbed up to look in the cupboard where we kept the cleaning supplies. Tile cleaner, bleach — and something wrapped in sparkly gold paper.

It was so beautiful I could hardly breathe. I pulled it out carefully. Was it for me? The wrapping paper was glossy and expensive-looking, with thin coils of burgundy ribbon. I'd never received a present wrapped like this.

No card was attached. It couldn't be for me, but it must be for me. There was only one way to find out.

I carried it over to the kitchen table. Should I open it? If I did, I'd have to be careful. I shook it and heard a little rattle.

No turning back. I was definitely going to open it. But how?

Maybe I could snip the tape at the side of the present, loosen the wrapping paper, and pull the box out. I found the kitchen scissors and slowly ran a blade along the first piece of tape. Gently, gently, I released it. Phew! One down, one to go.

Again, I slipped the sharp edge of the scissors along the tape. But this time, the scissors snagged on something. I tugged a little harder.

I watched in horror as the paper ripped down the side of the present.

Why had I taken the present out of the cupboard? If it *was* from Mom, she'd be hurt that I'd snooped. I couldn't let her know I'd tried to open it.

I set it on the table and noticed a little card under the wrapping paper. It said *Harley* — in Grandma's handwriting.

Then it was definitely for me. Grandma must have dropped it off early, knowing she wouldn't see us on Christmas Day. But that meant I was in deep trouble. Just what I needed — to have *both*

Mom and Grandma mad at me. I had to fix it before they realized what happened.

Now what? The paper was already ripped. I didn't have anything to lose by opening the present the rest of the way.

I slid off the ribbon and slipped the box out. It was gold with burgundy letters: *Vanderkley Jewellers*.

I held my breath as I tipped up the corner of the lid. Inside was a beautiful silver link bracelet with a heart charm. I lifted it out and held it in my hand. It was heavier than I expected. A couple of girls at school had bracelets like this, but those weren't nearly as pretty as this one. I draped it over my wrist, watching the heart dangle. *Harley* was engraved on one side.

Perfect.

I took off the bracelet and put it back. The box was the same colour as the wrapping paper. The store must have gift-wrapped my present in paper that matched the box.

The phone rang. I jumped.

"Hello, Harley."

It was Grandma.

I looked frantically around the kitchen. "Oh. Hi, Grandma," I said as I hid the present under a tea towel. She couldn't see me, but even so I didn't want to leave out the bracelet.

"I just called to tell you that you left your pencil case here."

I had gone over on Sunday to do some Internet research on Jacques Cartier. "I've been looking for it everywhere! Thanks, Grandma." My heart was pumping a thousand times a minute. I had to concentrate on not breathing too hard into the phone.

"I can drop it off tomorrow when I'm out shopping, but if you need it right away I'll come over tonight."

"Tomorrow's fine," I said. Imagine if Grandma came now!

"I won't keep you long, dear. I know it's almost dinner time. Good luck finishing your project, and we'll talk in a few days."

"Bye, Grandma."

Mom would be home in fifteen minutes. I

slipped the box back in the wrapping paper and retied the ribbon. It didn't look great, but good enough to pass if she was in the cleaning cupboard for something else.

I shoved the present to the back of the cupboard, ripped side against the wall. I moved the bleach in front of it, so Mom wouldn't see the rotten job I'd done on the ribbon. She cleaned the kitchen every night, but the bleach was saved for the big jobs she did on Saturday.

Time for some expert advice.

I called Naomi. Her family has call display, so I knew she'd see our name and answer in a silly way, like usual.

"Sam's Pickle Factory, Sam speaking," she said. I heard her mom in the background, singing "The Sound of Music" at the top of her lungs.

"Naomi, I need your help. I'm in the middle of a disaster."

"Is the house on fire?"

"I'm not kidding!"

"Neither am I. If the house is on fire, call 9-1-1. If not, let's talk. Actually, hold on."

Naomi put her hand over the receiver and her mom's voice got fainter. Then I heard a door shut. "Okay, I'm in my room now," said Naomi. "I can talk. What's up?"

"You know how I said I'd snoop around for a present?"

"Right."

"Well, I did."

"And?"

"And I was trying to open it, and I ripped the wrapping paper."

Naomi laughed. "That's not a disaster. Funny, but not a disaster. Your mom must have more wrapping paper. Just rewrap it."

"Wish I could. The present isn't from Mom, it's from Grandma. And she bought it at some fancy jewellery store — "

"You are so lucky!" Naomi screamed. "What did you get?"

"A bracelet, but that's not the point. Grandma bought the gift, and the store wrapped it for her. With their own fancy wrapping paper."

Naomi gasped. "You mean — "

"Yeah. I can't rewrap it without anyone knowing."

"Oh, shoot. That *is* a disaster. What are you gonna do?"

"I was hoping *you'd* tell me!"

Naomi thought for a minute. "Can you tell your mom?"

"No way!"

"Why don't you call your Grandma and ask her for help?"

"You know how Mom is about Grandma. If I asked Grandma for help, I'd be stuck right in the middle, right where I don't want to be."

"You know what you're going to have to do," said Naomi.

"What?"

"Go to the store and get it rewrapped."

"But Vanderkley's is downtown. I can't ask Mom to take me and not tell her why."

"You don't have to tell her. We'll go tomorrow during school."

It took me a minute to realize what she was saying.

"Skip school?"

"Sure! We'll call in sick, then go to the jewellery store. We'll be back before the end of the day, no problem."

Naomi could talk me into anything.

There was no other way — we would have to skip school. We planned to call in sick, take the subway downtown, go to Vanderkley's, and get the bracelet wrapped. Simple, right? "How about later in the week?" I said.

"No way," said Naomi. "It's tomorrow or never. Don't forget, the Holiday Pageant is Thursday. You told me your mom is coming to watch. She'd notice if you weren't there. And the class party's on Friday. We can't miss that!"

She was right. If we wanted to get the present rewrapped without getting caught, we'd have to go the next day.

4

I still had one thing to do. I opened the phone book to the "V" page. There it was: Vanderkley Jewellers.

I didn't stop to think. I dialled the number and listened to the ring. Three times, four times. Maybe they were closed. Maybe it was a sign that we shouldn't go downtown.

"Hello. Vanderkley Jewellers. How may I direct your call?"

What should I say? The lady on the phone sounded busy.

"Vanderkley Jewellers," she repeated.

I didn't want her to hang up. "Hi," I said, really fast.

There was a pause as we waited for each other to talk. "How may I direct your call?" she asked again.

Why didn't she speak in plain English? "Um, can I talk to someone about, uh, about this present I got? I mean, I didn't get it yet, but I'm going to get it for Christmas."

Smooth.

She said, "One moment, please," and I heard a click as she put me on hold. Classical music came on the line. I drummed my fingers and waited for someone to pick up.

"Customer Service. How may I help you?"

This time it was a man. He didn't sound any friendlier. I realized I couldn't explain my problem over the phone. I'd have to tell them when I was there.

"Um, if I wanted to go to your store, how would I get there?"

"We are located at 58 Bloor Street West."

I'd seen the address in the phone book. How did he think I got the phone number? "No, I mean, can I take the subway?"

"Take it to the Bloor/Yonge station, then walk two blocks west," he said. He was shuffling papers in the background. I scribbled down the directions.

"Will there be anything else?" he asked.

"Uh, no thanks," I said, and hung up. I folded the directions and tucked them in my pocket. Way too important to lose.

Just then Mom walked in the front door, her arms full of books. A couple of them slid off the top and I flinched as they hit the floor. "Give me a hand, Harley?"

I leaned over to pick up her books, hoping she wouldn't see my red face and guess something was up.

I set them beside the pile she had put on the kitchen counter. As I straightened, she gave me a funny look.

"What?" I said. Maybe I looked guilty.

"Nothing. Sometimes I can't believe how grown-up you are. I got you a baby doll for Christmas when you were two. It seems like yesterday. Guess I'll have to do better than a doll this year, won't I?"

My heart pounded. She *was* going to get me a gift! "It doesn't matter," I said cautiously. "No problem if we don't exchange presents." That was the biggest lie in the world.

Mom was searching for her favourite mug, the one with the lilies around the side. "What are you talking about?"

"Well, I know we're really broke."

She pulled her arm out of the cupboard and stared at me. "And?"

I twisted a strand of hair around my finger. "And I heard you talking to Aunt Heather on Saturday. You said you couldn't afford something. I thought maybe you meant Christmas."

She shook her head. "I've always managed to get you a Christmas present, and I always will."

"Good. Because I was lying when I said it didn't matter."

Mom smiled. "I know."

What was I thinking? Of course she'd get me a present.

"Sorry if you've been worried," she said. "I've

been so stressed out with other stuff that I've barely thought about Christmas." She sat down at the kitchen table. "In fact, can we talk? I have something to tell you."

Uh-oh. That didn't sound good. Still, she looked happy, so it couldn't be all bad. I sat down beside her.

"I meant to tell you a couple of weeks ago, but it's been crazy busy. And I still can't believe it myself." Mom pointed to the books she had carried in. "I'm thinking about going to college."

College? More school? Mom had finished high school part-time a couple of years ago. "Oh," I said, still twisting my hair.

"You're getting older now, and more responsible. You help so much around the house, and that makes something like this possible."

"What would you study?"

"I'd take a floral management course which would help me get a better job at a bigger shop. Maybe even start my own business one day." Mom's hair was in a ponytail, and her eyes were sparkling. She looked like the girl in the track picture.

"But college costs a lot of money," I said.

"That's what Heather and I were talking about. She told me to try for a bank loan. I went in yesterday and they said I'd qualify. I've been putting aside some money every week to help pay for tuition and materials, too."

"And that's why we've been broke this fall?"

"Right. But when I get my diploma, it'll really pay off." She paused. "What do you think?"

My happiness at hearing I'd be getting a Christmas present vanished. I bit my lip. "Already you don't get home from work until five-thirty. If you went back to school, I'd never see you."

"It'll be tough," said Mom, "but I'll only work part-time when I'm in school." She sat back in her chair. "I don't need to decide until after the holidays. But I wanted to let you know about it."

I didn't want to talk about it after the holidays, or ever. It was a terrible idea. "I don't care. I like things the way they are."

"Harley, we're in this together. And I can't do it without you. Just let yourself get used to the idea."

"Okay," I said. I knew I'd never get used to the idea.

She picked up the kitchen wipe and scrubbed a stain on the counter.

"Anyway, I'm glad we talked about Christmas. For sure I'm giving you a gift. I hope you didn't worry too much about it."

I thought about the ripped present and my plans for going downtown. I sighed. "No problem."

Mom stopped scrubbing the counter. "It's no use. I can't get this jam stain out."

Oops. I'd eaten my usual peanut-butter-and-blueberry-jam sandwich for breakfast. Guess I'd forgotten to wipe up before I left for school.

"If I leave this 'til the weekend, I'll never get it out," she said. She made a move for the cleaning cupboard.

Was she going to use the bleach? I had to stop her.

"No!" I shouted.

Mom paused, her hand on the cupboard door-knob. "What's up?"

My mind raced. What was a good reason?

Dinner wouldn't be ready for a few minutes. I tucked my hair behind my ear, stalling for time. "I, uh, oh I forgot to tell you. Grandma called a while ago."

"She did?" Mom took her hand off the knob.

I nodded. "I left my pencil case at her house. She'll drop it off tomorrow."

She looked puzzled. "Oh, okay." She reached up to the cupboard again.

"Wait!" I said. "The stain's my fault — I forgot to clean this morning. I'll work on the counter while you put your books away. It would be terrible if we spilled tuna casserole on them."

Mom laughed. "You're right. If you can't get it out, I'll try after dinner." She carried her books out of the kitchen.

I yanked a rag and cleaner out of the cupboard and scrubbed as hard as I could. Two things were clear — one, I was going to get that stain out; and two, I was definitely getting the present rewrapped. Tomorrow.

5

I reached in my pocket for the coins and dropped them in the fare box. They jingled as they hit the other loose change on the bottom. I wondered if the man in the booth would notice me and ask why I wasn't in school. But he motioned me through without looking up.

Naomi was way ahead of me, almost at the top of the escalator. "Hurry up!" she shouted, waving her arm. "I hear a train coming."

As I ran, I patted my other pocket to make sure the rest of my change was still there — enough to get back home, with extra for a treat downtown. I had promised Naomi I'd buy a snack, the least I could do since she was skipping school to come with me. If only I was more like her and could enjoy the day off. Playing hooky didn't seem to bother her at all.

We ran down the escalator two steps at a time and got to the bottom as the subway doors opened. A few people climbed off, but more of us got on. Naomi and I found seats together as the train started to move.

"Did you bring the directions?" she asked.

I checked my bag for the thirteenth time since breakfast. Yes, I had the directions — and the bracelet.

"They're here," I said. "Thank goodness. No way I'd call Vanderkley's again."

I looked at the subway map over the door. Nine more stops to Yonge station.

"So, let me see the bracelet," said Naomi.

"Not on the subway. I might lose it. Or someone might try to steal it."

"Get a hold of yourself. Who's gonna steal a bracelet at ten o'clock in the morning?"

I glanced around the subway car. Most of the other people were reading or sleeping. None of them looked like a jewel thief. I pulled the box out and tilted open the lid.

"Whoa!" said Naomi. "That is *so* gorgeous. Can I try it on?"

"Sorry." I shut the lid and put the box away. "I don't even want to touch it until it's officially mine."

"Your Grandma always comes through with the major gift. Do you think it's because she loves you, or because she knows it ticks off your mom?"

Good question. Mom never said anything about the presents Grandma gave me, but I could tell by the way she raised her eyebrow that she thought they were too expensive.

"I don't know, but Mom isn't in my good books right now."

"Did she find out about the bracelet?"

"No. She says she's going to college next year. Isn't that awful?"

"Why awful?" said Naomi.

"She's too busy already. If she goes to college, I'll never see her anymore. I have to figure out how to change her mind."

"It might be okay," she said. "If she gets a better job, you'll be able to buy more stuff, like a CD player. Or one of those sixty-inch plasma TVs."

I didn't say anything. A CD player would be great, but I didn't want more stuff. I wanted more Mom.

I settled back in my seat. I'd been so busy all morning — pretending I was leaving for school, calling in sick, sneaking to the subway — that this was my first chance to think about what we were doing. We were actually on our way downtown. I had thought I would chicken out, or someone would stop me on the way to the subway, or Mom would find the gift first. I started to giggle — I really couldn't believe what we were doing.

"What?" said Naomi.

I shook my head and laughed harder.

The lady sitting across the aisle peered at me over her glasses. She was knitting a green-and-white striped scarf that was already about three metres long. I was making too much noise for her liking. Maybe she knew we were skipping out of school. I stopped laughing.

I tried to imagine what everyone else was doing in transit in the middle of the morning. Like the man with a briefcase, working on a crossword puzzle. Shouldn't he be at work already?

I hardly ever rode the subway. The last time was for our class trip to City Hall and St. Lawrence Market. City Hall was boring, but I'd loved the market. It had that stinky cheese smell, and they sold weird things like fish with their eyes still in and live lobsters. I had wanted to buy one of the lobsters and set it free in Lake Ontario, but Naomi had said that would kill it for sure.

The doors opened and a new set of passengers got on. A girl with two nose rings sat across from us. She was wearing headphones, but the music was so loud we all heard it. She closed her eyes and bobbed her head to the music. The man with the briefcase glared at her. The woman with the scarf moved to the other end of the train.

Naomi nudged me and said, "Would you ever get your nose pierced?"

"No way!" I didn't even have the nerve to get my ears pierced. "What about you?"

"Ew! Think about it. How would you blow your nose?"

I didn't want to think about it that much.

The subway car was getting crowded. A woman sat down on the other side of Naomi, and now we were squashed in our seats. I started to wish we hadn't come.

"Naomi, we should turn around and go home."

She didn't move, didn't say a word. She was looking away from me.

"Let's get off at the next station and get on a train going back," I said. "If we hurry, we'll get to school before lunch. We'll make up a story about being late, and no one will ever know."

Naomi still didn't move. I shifted forward to see what she was doing.

The lady next to her was reading *The National Enquirer*. Naomi was leaning over her shoulder, reading an article called "The Loch Ness Monster — Fact or Fiction?"

"Don't read that stuff," I whispered. "You know it's all made up."

She turned to me. "No, they have proof that the

Loch Ness monster exists. There's even a picture!"

The train stopped and a lady with a cane hobbled on. I didn't see anywhere for her to sit. The subway began to move.

The girl with the nose rings stood up. She lowered her headphones onto her shoulders and the music blared through the subway train.

"Awful noise," muttered the man with the newspaper. Loch Ness Lady shook her head.

"Would you like my seat?" asked Nose Rings.

The woman with the cane eased herself into the seat. "Thank you, dear. That's very kind."

Nose Rings put her headphones back on. Her music was still loud enough for the rest of us to hear, but nobody complained. The train was packed now, and I checked for the fourteenth time — the bracelet and directions were still there. I was getting crease marks in my hand from holding the plastic bag tightly.

All these people. It was weird how you could live in a city, or ride a subway, with so many people and not feel connected to any of them. Was there anyone out there like me?

"St. George station!" the conductor announced.

About a hundred people stepped off, including Loch Ness Lady. The man with the crossword puzzle left his newspaper on the seat.

"He's littering," said Naomi. "I feel like getting off and giving his paper back to him."

"No," I said. "We still have two more stops. I don't want to walk that far."

A crowd of people pushed on the train. I closed my eyes, and collapsed back in my seat. I felt like I'd done a day's work already, and it was only ten-thirty. Compared to this, school was relaxing.

I had forgotten about getting off the train and going back home, and it was too late now. We were nearly downtown, so we'd might as well go to Vanderkley's after all. We'd be done in fifteen minutes, tops. I looked again at the map over the door and elbowed Naomi. "Our station's next."

"That was fun!" she said. "We should take the subway more often!"

I took her arm as I checked my bag one more

time for the bracelet and directions. "Thanks for coming. I could never do this by myself!"

The problem was, I didn't know if I could do it with Naomi's help, either.

6

When we climbed off the subway, we found ourselves in an underground shopping mall. People were hurrying by us, and a line of stores stretched out in both directions. There had to be a door somewhere that led outside, but I didn't know how to find it.

"I'm lost," I said.

"I know where we are!" said Naomi. "I came with Dad when he was writing an article about cameras. We're right under the Bay. Let's go through the store."

She led me over to the escalators and we rode up.

"Excuse me," a voice said as we reached the

main floor of the Bay. A saleslady wearing a white lab coat and snowman earrings wobbled over on her high heels. "Would you like to try Passion's Embrace?"

I had no idea what she was talking about, until I saw the bottle of perfume she held in her hand.

Naomi said, "I hate perfume."

I hesitated. The saleslady must think I was pretty grown-up if she wanted me to try it. "Sure," I said. I pushed my coat sleeve up my arm. "Spray away."

She held the bottle an inch from my wrist and squeezed. Suddenly, my arm was soaked in Passion's Embrace.

"Do you like it?"

"It's okay," I said, not wanting her to expect me to buy the perfume. I shoved my sleeve up to my elbow. I didn't want it to get drenched, too.

"If you buy today, you'll get a free gift." She pointed to a little table stacked with candy-cane–striped makeup bags.

"I'll think about it," I said, backing away. The saleslady turned to find a new victim.

Naomi stepped away from me and held her nose. "You smell awful. That's even worse than my mom's perfume. It smells like when you forget about bananas in the cupboard."

My arm was still shiny from where I'd been hit. I brought it closer to my nose and sniffed. I coughed. Naomi was right.

"I smell like Rosa Schultz," I said. Rosa lived at the end of our street. Mom said she was wild.

"All you need are some tall boots and a short skirt, and you'd *be* Rosa Schultz."

I made a face. "Let's find a bathroom. I need to wash it off."

After I'd scrubbed my arm with lots of soap and water, we walked out of the Bay onto Bloor Street. As far as I could see, the street lamps were decorated with clusters of holly and strands of tiny yellow lights.

"I forgot how cold it is outside," said Naomi, zipping up her coat.

I pulled my gloves out of my plastic bag. Thank goodness I'd packed them. I'd only thrown them in at the last minute because Mom was making a big deal about the temperature. I wanted to stop and put them on, but everyone was walking so fast. I tugged Naomi's arm and pulled her over beside one of the stores.

"Why is everyone in such a hurry?" I asked. "And where are they going?"

"Beats me," said Naomi. "I guess they all have important jobs."

I clutched the gloves under my arm while I tugged at my coat zipper. I tugged too fast.

"Oh, no, it's broken," I said.

I held the useless zipper tag in my left hand and watched the crowd walk by: short people, tall people, people in boots and people in shoes, people talking on their cell phones and people talking to themselves. Had everyone in the city come to Bloor Street today? "They all look like they know where they're going, but I'm lost."

"Don't you have the directions?"

"Yeah, but I'm not sure which way is east and which is west." My stomach was hurting, my hand was cramping from holding the bag, and I didn't know which way to go.

I was so busy staring at the slip of paper with the directions, I didn't notice the man until he spoke to me.

"You look like you're lost. Can I help you?"

He was sitting on an overturned red milk crate, a sheet of blue plastic covering his lap and hanging over his legs. He had a blanket wrapped around his shoulders. I tried not to stare. I wondered if he was dangerous. "Maybe," I said hesitantly.

He grinned and showed a couple of gaps where teeth used to be. "Don't worry about me. Maybe I don't smell great, but I know this part of town like the back of my hand."

"Are you a homeless person?" asked Naomi.

I turned to her and whispered, "Don't!" But he just laughed.

"The sidewalk's my home," he said. He shook his hat, jingling the coins in it. "Spare change?" he called as a group of people walked by. They didn't answer him. They didn't even look at him.

He had long hair and a shaggy beard, and I had to breathe through my mouth so I wouldn't smell him. I still wasn't sure if I should talk to him, but who else would I ask? "How do I get to Vanderkley's?" I said.

He jerked his head to the left. "It's a couple of blocks that way. That's a pretty expensive store for a couple of young ladies to shop in. Why are you going there?"

"It's sort of a long story. I did something I wasn't supposed to, and now I have to fix things."

He nodded. "Sounds like a mission. Good luck to you. Hope they don't eat you alive."

Naomi tugged my arm. "Let's go, Harley."

"Right," I said. "Thanks," I called over my shoulder as she pulled me down the street.

"Have a nice day," he said.

Naomi locked her arm in mine. "I can't believe you asked him for directions."

I knew what she meant, but he was the first person I'd seen today that I felt connected to. I didn't fit in down here and neither did he. "It's such a cold day. I hope he's okay."

"Forget about him," said Naomi. "Look at us! We're downtown in the middle of the day. Have you ever seen such fantastic clothes?"

It was true. The woman walking toward us wore a long black coat with a matching hat, and boots with the highest heels I'd ever seen.

"If I had boots like that, I couldn't take two steps," I said. "But I love the hat."

"If I had boots like that, I'd never take them off," said Naomi.

We stopped at a red light. "What do you think he meant when he said, 'Hope they don't eat you alive'?" I asked.

She shrugged. "Maybe one time he tried to go in and they wouldn't let him. Would you want him in your house?"

"I guess not."

I looked back at the homeless man, who was still shaking his hat. Where did he go at night? Did he have somewhere to keep his stuff, or to shower? Did he ever have a house?

If Mom lost her job, would we have to live on the street? I shivered. I was pretty sure that Mom would always find a way.

The light turned green and we crossed the

street with a huge pack of people. I wondered if anyone else was going to Vanderkley's, and if they were as nervous as I was. Based on the phone call, I thought the salespeople really *might* eat me alive.

A bunch of people were standing in front of a building, smoking.

"Wow," I said. "You'd have to like smoking a lot to come outside on a day like today."

"I'll never smoke," said Naomi. "I'd rather spend my money on chocolate bars and CDs."

We walked by a lady in a uniform ringing a bell beside a big pot. "I wonder what she's doing," I said.

"Salvation Army," said Naomi. "They collect cash for poor people."

Maybe the homeless man would get some.

Naomi stopped in the middle of the sidewalk and grabbed my arm. "Hey! An HMV store!"

The bright pink sign hung over the sidewalk above us. A Christmas tree covered in white angel decorations and silver CDs filled the front window.

"We *have* to go in," Naomi said.

"Naomi — "

"Only for a minute, I promise. We can use the listening stations."

I wanted to get to the jewellery store as soon as possible. But I hardly ever went to HMV, and I wanted to try out the listening stations, too. Naomi reached for the door. She was going in with or without me.

"Okay," I said, following her in. "But then we're going *straight* to Vanderkley's."

Inside the store, "Hey Jude" was playing.

Naomi rolled her eyes. "Just like my mom. Will grown-ups *ever* get over the Beatles?"

To the right of the front door were three listening stations, and they were all free. "Let's go for it," I said.

Naomi stopped at the first one. "Cool!" she said. "F-Rod! I'm going to check him out."

"You can't listen to him! He's really bad!"

"How do you know he's bad?"

"Mom told me his songs are awful. He sings about terrible things!"

"I'll tell you what I think when I'm done," said Naomi, putting on the headphones.

I may have been miles away from home, but I was *not* going to listen to F-Rod. I put on the next set of headphones and pushed the button for the Maddie McDermott CD.

"I WANT YOUR LOVE ..."

Ouch! Way too loud!

"... TODAY, TONIGHT, TO — " I struggled with the headphones and pulled them off as fast as I could. I checked the volume control; it was at the max. I turned it down, then looked around to see if anyone had noticed. I tried again. Way better. During the first song, I imagined I was in the front row at one of Maddie's concerts. I pretended she asked me to come onstage with her and sing a duet.

Naomi was having a great time listening to F-Rod. She was singing out loud with the music, and a couple of teenagers by the information desk were laughing. I elbowed her.

"WHAT?" she shouted. She must be on max volume, too.

I pointed to the door with my thumb.

"LET ME FINISH THE SONG," she screamed, and started singing again.

I noticed two store employees looking at us and talking to each other. The taller one started down the escalator toward us. He must have guessed we were skipping school. Was he going to report us? I grabbed Naomi's arm.

"JUST A SEC," she said, waving me off.

The sales clerk was getting closer, and he was still looking at us. I waved my arms in front of Naomi's face.

Finally, she hung up the headphones. "Sweet!" she said. "I wonder if Mom would let me get that CD."

"We have to go," I hissed and pointed to the clerk. "I think he's onto us!" Naomi gasped and we tore out of the store.

Time to get down to business. I looked ahead and saw the burgundy and gold sign half a block away.

Vanderkley Jewellers.

7

"Here we are," Naomi said.

We stood on the sidewalk in front of Vanderkley's, looking up at the storefront. Two tall windows surrounded an enormous mahogany door with a gold handle. The window on the left had a display of burgundy vases and white poinsettias. The one on the right was filled with green wreaths draped in gold necklaces and earrings.

"Wow," I said. I swallowed hard. No more delays, no more excuses. "Let's get it over with. I'll do all the talking, Naomi. Don't even think of saying a word."

"Who, me?" said Naomi, smirking.

I breathed deeply and pulled the front-door

handle. The door was heavy, though, an.
open it only halfway. Naomi laughed,
made me laugh, and I let the door go. We s.
there laughing until a man in a grey suit walked
out carrying a Vanderkley's shopping bag. He
held the door open for us but the way he looked
at me, I felt like we should have stayed in HMV.
Maybe he noticed that my zipper was broken.

I'd never been in a store like Vanderkley's. We
paused in the lobby and admired a Christmas
tree, as high as the ceiling. It was covered in
sparkly gold bells and burgundy bows.

"I'll be right back," Naomi said, wandering
over to a display of crystal animals.

I pushed my hair out of my eyes and glanced
in one of the glass cases as if I was going to buy
something. The first thing I saw was a tiara. Who
would buy a tiara? I looked at the price tag and
gasped.

Why did I bring my bracelet in a No Frills
bag?

"May I help you?"

It took me a few seconds to realize the

saleslady was talking to me. Her hair was long, straight and blonde. She wore a navy dress and a brooch in the shape of a starfish, its golden tentacles dotted with tiny sapphires. Her fingernails were white at the tips and smooth across the top, not all jagged like mine. She could wear the tiara in the display case. Even in that plain navy dress, she was a real princess.

I tried to remember who I spoke to yesterday on the phone. "Oh, yeah. Where's Customer Service?"

The Princess wrinkled her nose. Did she smell my Passion's Embrace? "Down the stairs and straight ahead," she said. She turned to another customer, one who *did* look like he belonged in the store.

I wished I was invisible — or dead. Naomi came over, grinning.

"Look at that camel," she said. She pointed to a huge crystal camel that must have weighed a ton. "Guess how much it costs?" she asked, then didn't give me a chance to answer. "Seven thousand dollars! Who would pay that much?"

"Beats me — a wise man?" I took her arm. "Let's go downstairs now, before I change my mind."

"I wonder what they have down there. Eight-thousand-dollar llamas?"

"Shhh!" I said, but it was too late. The Princess stopped chatting with the man as Naomi's voice boomed through the store.

I couldn't look at Naomi, knowing I'd laugh if I did. Even with my back turned I felt the Princess staring at us. She didn't talk to her customer again until we were on our way downstairs.

We stifled our laughter until we were about halfway down, then we stopped to let it out. I was laughing so hard my stomach hurt.

When I caught my breath, I said, "Naomi, you *have* to be good." She crossed her eyes and we started laughing again.

I knew we were being too loud. "This place is like a library," I whispered.

Customer Service was against the back wall in the basement. We passed a cabinet full of silver bracelets, rings, and earrings. I hadn't seen that much bling since F-Rod's last music video.

"Check this out," said Naomi. She was looking at some rings and pendants at the counter beside the stairs. "This is all birthstone jewellery. My birthstone's emerald." She pointed to a necklace with little emeralds all the way down and a big one in the middle. "If I could buy any of them, I'd get this one. What's your birthstone?"

"Topaz."

"Topaz? What colour is that?"

"Yellow." I was so busy searching for a topaz ring, I didn't hear the salesman coming up behind me.

"Ladies. May I help you?"

I jumped. I still hadn't decided what to say.

"Can I try on this necklace?" asked Naomi.

"Actually, I need to talk to someone in Customer Service," I said.

"That would be me. How may I help you?"

He wore a uniform — a perfectly pressed white shirt with a name tag that said *Basil*, and navy pants with creases sharp enough to cut a diamond.

I reached into my bag and pulled out the present. "I think my grandma bought this here."

Basil took the box from me. "That's our box, and our wrapping paper." He opened it and lifted out the bracelet. "Is there a problem?" he asked.

I felt my face go red. "The thing is — it's a Christmas gift. I wanted to see what was inside, and I …"

He sighed. "Let me guess. You tore the wrapping paper while you were opening it. And you would like me to rewrap the gift so your grandmother doesn't know what you did."

I nodded, biting my lip.

"Fine. But you get one rewrap. If you rip it again, you're on your own." Basil frowned at the No Frills bag in my hand and said, "I'll take that, too." He grasped it with the tips of his thumb and forefinger and held it away from his body, like he was afraid he'd catch the plague from touching it.

He marched behind the Customer Service counter, flicking the bag into the garbage on the way. He leaned over the desk and spoke to a woman sitting behind it. Her hair was pulled back from her face so tightly it must have hurt. He gestured in my direction and they both looked up at me. Neither of them smiled.

Naomi snorted. "I bet that woman lives in a freezer."

She could live at the South Pole for all I cared, as long as she was wrapping my gift.

"I wonder if there's anything in here I could afford," said Naomi.

"I saw some pens over there," I said. I wanted to keep my eye on the bracelet, but Naomi went over and peered in.

"Five hundred dollars!" shouted Naomi. "That pen costs five hundred dollars!"

Freezer Lady looked up from the desk. Her forehead was full of wrinkle lines, the mad kind. I thought she might zap me into a block of ice with her eyes.

"Who would pay five hundred dollars for a pen?" asked Naomi.

"Oh, it's not a pen," I said, pointing to the sign in the display. "It's a *Writing Instrument*."

"What's the difference between a pen and a writing instrument?"

"About four hundred and ninety-nine dollars."

What was I doing in a store like this? At least they were rewrapping the gift. In five minutes we'd be out the door. Nothing could go wrong now.

"Harley? Harley, is that you?"

I froze. The voice came from behind my back, which meant it wasn't Basil or Freezer Lady. And it sure didn't sound like Naomi. I turned slowly to find myself face-to-face with Ethel Everhart.

"I barely recognized you," she said. "You're getting so tall!" She sniffed. "Are you wearing perfume?"

What were the chances of me running into Grandma's next-door neighbour on the one day I skipped school? "Hello, Mrs. Everhart."

She frowned and peered at me. "Aren't you supposed to be in school?"

"Uh, no, we're downtown today," I said, hoping she wouldn't ask for details.

She scowled. "This new curriculum! They've really changed field trips since my girls were in school." She shook her head. "I must be on my way. Have a good Christmas."

"Thank you, Mrs. Everhart. You too," I called as she shuffled over to the stairs.

"Who was that?" Naomi hissed.

I closed my eyes. "I am so dead. She's Grandma's neighbour. What if she tells her she saw me?"

"Relax," Naomi said. "She probably won't say anything. Besides, the good news is — your present's ready."

Freezer Lady strode over and handed me a burgundy Vanderkley's bag. "We've rewrapped your present," she said. "You're all set to go." She even looked like she was trying to smile, but I didn't buy it.

"Thank you," I said, my stomach still churning. "Let's go," I whispered to Naomi.

When we reached the top of the stairs, Naomi said, "Are you still worried about that lady?"

"Mrs. Everhart? She was barely halfway up the stairs when Freezer Lady gave me the gift. What if she heard? I just want to get out of here." I was too scared to be happy that the present looked like new. "I can't believe we skipped school today. If our parents ever find out, we're in huge trouble."

"They'll never find out." But Naomi sounded less confident than usual.

We pushed the front door together and opened it on the first try. I took a deep breath, enjoying my freedom. For once, the cold air was a relief.

"Don't forget you promised to buy muffins," said Naomi.

The muffin shop was on our way to the subway station. We passed the homeless man again, and he winked at me.

"I remember you! Mission accomplished?"

I nodded. I stuck my hand in my pocket and felt the extra change in there. Maybe I could give it to him. Naomi and I didn't really need muffins …

"I'm starving!" said Naomi. "If I don't eat right now, I'm going to die!"

Before I knew it, we were in the muffin shop. I bought two chocolate-chip muffins. On our way out I glanced over my shoulder. The homeless man was turned the other way, shaking his hat at the crowds walking by. I hoped he would stay warm.

"Let's save the muffins and eat them at your place," said Naomi.

"Sure," I said, but I was nervous about going home. What if someone saw us before school was out? I could say I was sick, but that wouldn't explain Naomi. She had to hide out at my place until four o'clock because her dad worked from their house.

I shivered and pulled my coat tightly around myself. Time to go home and hope for the best.

8

We got back to my place with no problem. If it had been warmer, Mr. Simpson across the street probably would have seen us. Now that he was retired, he spent most of his time on his front porch and chatting to the neighbours. But it was too cold even for Mr. Simpson. After Naomi went home — late enough that her dad wouldn't ask questions — I started dinner.

And I worked extra hard on my homework to make up for missing school. If I never read anything about Jacques Cartier again, it would be too soon. My head was swimming with thoughts of scurvy and failed attempts to find the Northwest Passage.

Mom was in the living room hemming a pair of pants for me. My winter coat sat beside her — she had fixed the zipper as soon as she got home. It looked as good as new. Mom lifted her head and smiled at me.

"Almost done, kiddo. Try on the pants after dinner."

"Thanks."

If we had lots of money, I'd go to American Eagle and buy whatever I wanted. But no way could we afford it. Anyway, Naomi always said no one would guess that most of my clothes were second-hand. At least Mom found good stuff at the consignment and vintage stores and knew how to alter it. You could always spot the kids who got their clothes from Goodwill.

Mom leaned back in her chair and stretched. "I'll set the table. Your chicken smells delicious." The phone rang. She picked it up and a moment later handed it to me, saying, "It's for you. Your grandmother."

"Hi, Grandma!"

"Hi, Harley. I left your pencil case in your

mailbox this morning. Did you find it?"

Hard to believe it was only a day since I talked to her, the torn paper and the bracelet on the counter in front of me. "I did, thanks. The pencil case was freezing when I brought it in. I had to let the markers warm up before I used them!"

"Harley, I'd like to speak to you in private for a minute."

Mom was getting the milk out of the fridge, not paying attention to my side of our conversation. "Sure," I said, taking the phone into my room. This didn't sound good. "Okay, I'm alone now. What's up?"

"Do you have something you need to tell me?"

Mom said the same thing when I was about to get in trouble. She must have got all her lines from Grandma. "Um, about what?" I stalled.

"About your Christmas present."

I felt like a balloon losing its air. "What do you mean?" I asked. I didn't want to give anything away, in case she was guessing.

"Ethel called me this afternoon. She said she

83

ran into you at Vanderkley's and overheard something about getting a present rewrapped?"

"Oh." I was nailed.

"You and your mother are like two peas in a pod. This is the kind of thing she'd have done when she was your age. Do you realize how dangerous your trip downtown could have been?"

"Yes, Grandma."

"Never skip school again, and never, ever go downtown without an adult. If you do, I'll tell your mother, and your school principal, and anyone else who needs to know."

"Yes, Grandma."

"Then we'll leave it at that." She chuckled. "It would serve your mother right if you gave her as much trouble growing up as she gave me."

What did Grandma mean when she said we were like two peas in a pod? I wasn't like Mom at all. Mom was brave and strong, and she wasn't afraid of anything.

She continued, "I'd love it if you could come over to help me decorate my Christmas tree. Are you free Friday evening?"

"I think so. Let me check with Mom." Every year, Grandma put up two Christmas trees, one in the living room at the front of the house and a smaller one in the den at the back. She decorated the big tree by herself, but she usually let me help with the other one.

I ran out to the kitchen. "Can I go to Grandma's house on Friday? She wants me to help decorate her tree."

"Sure. Give me the phone and I'll work out the details."

I handed her the phone.

As I went into the living room, I heard Mom talking in a low voice. Every one of her sentences was about three words long, and probably Grandma's were too. Why couldn't they just talk to each other?

I looked out the front window. Most of the houses had Christmas lights. Mr. and Mrs. Simpson had green and red lights strung around their front door, their bushes, and their mailbox. They also had statues of Santa and Mrs. Claus, and all the reindeer with a sleigh full of plastic presents. Some people thought the Simpsons' decorations were tacky, but I loved how they celebrated the holidays. Their sons and daughters and all their grandchildren came over for dinner, and it always seemed like their house would burst with joy. Why couldn't my family be more like them? I wished Mom and Grandma got along. I wished the three of us could have Christmas dinner together.

Mom was hanging up the phone when I joined her at the kitchen table. "She'll pick you up Friday night at five-thirty. I'll be home by then to see you off." She slid into her chair. "The chicken smells awesome. I can't wait to try it."

"You look tired, Mom."

"I'm okay. Life's busy right now."

How did Mom think she was going to do all of this plus school? "You'll be busier if you take that course."

"We'll manage," she said.

I was tired of thinking about money. And I was tired of Mom being brave all the time. I just wanted to put my head down and cry.

"I don't want to manage. I want things to stay the same."

"I know. But things never stay the same. I've dreamed about going back to school, and now it looks like it's going to happen."

"What about *me*? I'll be in grade seven next year and I'll have even more homework. You won't be here to help me at all. I miss you when you're not here."

"I miss you, too," said Mom, her voice breaking. "But it's the only way."

I pushed my plate away and set my fork down. "I'm sick of being poor. I'm sick of wearing second-hand clothes, and not having a CD player, and worrying about money all the time. I don't care about your dreams."

Mom looked hurt. "I hope you don't really mean that. All I know is that, after I take this course, I can get a better-paying job. And then things will get easier."

I hated how she had an answer for everything. I stood up. "I'm not hungry anymore," I said, shoving my chair away from the table. I stalked off to my room.

Mom called, "Harley, wait a minute," but I ignored her. Enough talking. I wanted to be by myself.

9

Friday was the last day before Christmas holidays, so there was no homework. I'd gone to Naomi's house after school and we listened to some of my new CDs. We played Maddie McDermott's new single at least eight times. I gave Naomi the F-Rod CD that Frank had brought.

Mom and I both got home just before five-thirty and I was running around, getting ready to go to Grandma's. Since our fight two days earlier, Mom had tried to talk to me about her college plans, but I would change the subject or just ignore her. Mom didn't realize how much I'd miss her. It was bad enough that I had to come home to an empty house. Why couldn't I have a normal life with my mom home with me?

Grandma pulled in the driveway. "Just a sec," said Mom. "Wear your boots." She reached around the landing to the basement and grabbed them. "Carry your shoes and put them on when you get there."

Wearing boots made me feel like a little kid, but Grandma was ringing the doorbell, and it wasn't a good time to argue. I shoved my feet in the boots as Mom answered the door.

"Hi, Grandma!" I said as I let her in.

Grandma always looked like she came right from the hairdresser, every hair shiny and falling exactly right. Mom told me once that Grandma had been dying her hair so long that nobody could remember its original colour.

Mom hugged me, then looked up at Grandma. "When will you bring her back?"

"When we're done," said Grandma. Mom lifted an eyebrow. I prayed silently that they wouldn't fight. Then Grandma added, "Maybe eight-thirty or nine."

Mom rolled her eyes. "Fine," she said.

It seemed like they'd squeezed everything they could out of that conversation. I followed Grandma out of the house.

I felt like a celebrity when I rode in her car. It had heated seats that kept your bum warm in the winter and a sun roof that Grandma never opened. She had one of her Mozart CDs in the player that held more CDs than I owned. It was hard to sing along with Mozart. Too bad Grandma didn't like Maddie McDermott.

Grandma pulled out of the driveway and I gripped the armrest. She was a grandmother, but she drove that fancy car too fast.

"How was your report card?" asked Grandma.

"Pretty good. I even got a B+ in math."

Grandma looked happy. She knew math wasn't easy for me. "Did you finish your Jacques Cartier project?" She made a quick left-hand turn, and I slid across the leather seat toward the car door.

I nodded and yanked myself up straight again. "It was due today. I worked hard — I'm glad I'm done! Thanks for your help, Grandma."

"You're welcome to use my computer any time you want."

"Mom might be going to college next year," I blurted. Why did I tell her that? If she disapproved, she might call Mom and lecture her. Wouldn't Mom be thrilled about that! But Grandma looked happy. "That would be wonderful."

I didn't know what to say. Mom and Grandma didn't agree on anything. Figures they'd agree on the one thing I didn't want to happen. Didn't anyone care about my feelings?

As we got closer to Grandma's, the houses were bigger and farther apart, with expensive Christmas decorations. No Santa statues here. Her next-door neighbours chose a different colour scheme every year, and hired someone to decorate the huge trees in the front yard. This year their lights were blue and the ivy garlands draped around their house had blue and gold bows.

Grandma had a double row of white lights around her roof and a huge silver and white wreath on the front door. She loved gardening, like Mom, and her yard was full of plants. Some of the bushes were wrapped in burlap and twine. They would stay covered until spring to protect them from the cold.

The car jolted to a stop in her driveway. "Careful where you walk," Grandma said. "The sidewalk's slippery."

She was wearing high-heeled boots just like that lady on Bloor Street. As she picked her way to the door I thought, *I don't care what Naomi says. I am never going to wear boots like that!*

Every time I went to Grandma's house I had to pinch myself. I knew it was huge and bright and full of new furniture, but it still amazed me. Hard to believe I was related to someone who had a grandfather clock in the front hall and a living room the same size as our whole house.

Grandma handed me a hanger. "Put your coat away and change into your shoes while I order the pizza. Join me in the den when you're ready."

Pizza was a treat, since Mom and I hardly ever ordered in. Grandma knew what I liked — double cheese with pepperoni — and that's what she always ordered, even though she didn't like pepperoni. In fact, she didn't really like pizza. But she knew I loved it.

A scent of fresh pine filled the air. I glanced into the living room and saw the biggest Christmas tree ever. Grandma's formal tree looked like a picture from a magazine, with all the ornaments in silver and white. The star at the top reflected the chandelier lights across the walls. I felt like I was back in Vanderkley's.

Grandma's other tree was in the den at the back of the house, and she'd already strung the lights on it. Boxes of ornaments were neatly stacked to the right of the TV stand. "Time to decorate," she said.

We had just opened the second box of decorations when I pulled out a golden bell. I had never looked at it closely before, but this year I noticed the burgundy trim around the bottom and a "V" engraved on the inside.

"Did you get this at Vanderkley's, Grandma?"

"Yes, I did. I forgot how well you know their merchandise."

"We have one like this, too," I said.

Grandma didn't say anything.

"Did you buy it for us?"

"You were just over a month old on your first Christmas. I bought these ornaments to celebrate your birth, one for us and one for your mother. She hung hers on this tree every year until she moved out."

"Now she hangs it on our tree every year," I said.

"I'm glad she likes it. It means a lot to me, too."

I pulled out a snowman that was crumbling around the edges. "Should I throw this out, Grandma?"

"Your mother made it in grade three. It's been falling apart for fifteen years, but I can't imagine putting up a tree without it."

I gently placed it on a low branch. "Tell me a story about when Mom was a little kid."

Grandma took her arm out of the decorations box and sat back to think. "She looked up to her big sister. But Heather was four years older and didn't always want to play with her." She smiled.

"I remember one summer Heather and her best friend set up a booth at the end of our lane and sold lemonade to the neighbours. They wouldn't let your mother help because they thought she was a baby. She was about six years old. She got so angry, she put up her own booth next to theirs and took out a bag of cookies to sell. Of course, anyone who stopped for lemonade had to buy cookies, too." Grandma laughed. "By the end of the day she made as much money as Heather and her friend, but she didn't have to split her profits with anyone."

I hadn't heard that story before. That sounded exactly like Mom.

Grandma hung a cross-stitched poinsettia, then stood back to inspect the tree. "Your mother is very stubborn. Sometimes that's a good thing and sometimes it isn't."

I pretended to concentrate on hanging a little wooden sleigh. "Is that why you guys don't talk to each other?" I asked casually.

"I suppose so," said Grandma.

"Was it because of me?"

"When you were born, I was thrilled. You were my first grandchild. I couldn't wait to see you."

"But Mom had to quit high school." I didn't want to ask the next question but I had to know the answer. "Were your fights worse after I was born?"

"Absolutely not!" Grandma took my hand. "We finally had something in common when you were born — we both loved you like crazy."

I squeezed her hand, my heart pounding. I was still the only thing they had in common. Getting them together was up to me. "If Mom wanted to be friends again, would you?"

Grandma looked at me, surprised. "Harley …"

"Would you want to be friends again?"

The doorbell rang.

Grandma went to get the pizza. I wished the delivery man hadn't come at that moment. Still, she hadn't said no right away — maybe there was hope for her and Mom.

We finished hanging the last few decorations, then sat in the dining room to eat. Grandma said,

"Are you looking forward to Christmas, Harley?"

"Yeah." She raised her eyebrows at me. "I mean, yes. We're going to Naomi's house on Boxing Day."

I didn't know what else to say. Christmas Day would be quiet — just Mom and me. We would open our presents after breakfast, work on a jigsaw puzzle all afternoon, then watch "White Christmas" after a turkey dinner.

"That sounds nice." She picked the pepperoni off her pizza with a fork.

"Are you going to Aunt Heather's house?" I asked. Grandma always had Christmas dinner with Aunt Heather and her family.

"No. This year they're visiting Mike's family in Ottawa. I'll see them when they get back on the twenty-seventh."

"Then what are you doing on Christmas?"

"I'll go to church in the morning, then spend a quiet day here."

I set my milk glass down on the table a little too hard. Grandma winced but didn't say anything. "You can't be by yourself on Christmas day," I said. "Come over to our place. You can have Christmas dinner with us!"

As soon as the words were out of my mouth, I realized one good thing and one bad thing about the invitation. The good thing was this — maybe I had found a way to get Mom and Grandma together. The bad thing was this — I'd never seen them in the same room for more than half an hour.

Still, maybe it would work.

She didn't move. "Maybe you should run this invitation by your mother first."

She didn't say no!

I crossed my fingers behind my back. "Mom would love to have you over. She was just saying that Christmas day is too quiet."

Grandma finished her slice of pizza and put her napkin beside the plate. "If your mother agrees, I'd be happy to join you for dinner on the twenty-fifth."

10

It had seemed so simple. Invite Grandma, and she'll have Christmas dinner with us!

I hadn't thought about how I'd ask Mom.

That night I told myself it was too late to talk when I got home from Grandma's house, but in reality I hadn't known what to say. Now I needed to ask Mom. Christmas was in two days and we planned to buy our groceries this afternoon.

I cleared my throat. "Wouldn't it be fun to have more people over for Christmas dinner?"

"Maybe," said Mom. She wasn't really listening. She had one of her school brochures out and was reading about the courses.

I ran my hand across the table. Spotless.

"What if we invited Grandma for dinner on Christmas day?"

Mom stopped reading. "What did you say?"

I gulped. "Well, I mentioned to Grandma that maybe she could have dinner here on the twenty-fifth. Is that okay?"

Mom looked at me like I'd said, "I want to have Christmas dinner on Mount Kilimanjaro." She stood up and stacked her schoolbooks in a pile. "That isn't a very good idea, Harley. Let's clear the table and have some lunch. We should finish the tin of tuna in the fridge."

She wasn't going to distract me that easily. "Why isn't it a good idea?" I asked.

"There's too much history. I wish I could wave a magic wand and make things different, but I can't."

Time to lay on the guilt. "You know Aunt Heather's going to Ottawa this Christmas. I thought Grandma might be lonely."

Mom sighed. "You're so thoughtful. I just don't know if I can do it."

She hadn't said no! I felt a burst of energy as I

realized my plan might actually work. "What if Grandma said she'd come?"

Mom was pulling carrots and celery out of the vegetable crisper. She turned around to look at me. "Did she?"

"She said she would, if it was all right with you."

Mom didn't say anything. She crossed her arms and tilted her head to one side, like she always does when she's thinking about something.

I continued. "I promise I'll cook the whole meal. You won't have to do anything."

"It's not the food I'm worried about."

"What if this was my Christmas present?"

"What do you mean?"

"You don't have to buy me anything for Christmas. All I want is dinner with you and Grandma." Not exactly true. But it sounded good.

"Don't be ridiculous." Mom uncrossed her arms and put one hand on her hip. She hesitated, then said, "Would having your grandmother to dinner mean that much to you?"

I nodded.

"We'll see." She went back to the fridge.

Mom was going to think about it. And for now, that was enough.

As we sat down for lunch, I had a great idea. If Grandma was happy about Mom going back to school, she might offer to pay our bills. Then Mom wouldn't have to work at all.

I asked Mom, "Why don't you borrow the money from Grandma instead of from the bank?"

"No way. We've fought too much about money."

Even though I hardly ever pushed Mom on things, I was tired of her ignoring my feelings. "But it's okay if you're too busy to spend any time with me?"

"I said we'd discuss it after the holidays. You've asked me to make one big decision about your grandmother — I can't handle anything else right now."

She had a point. There would be lots of time for me to change her mind about college in the new year.

Mom didn't say much for the rest of the meal. After lunch, I went into the bathroom to brush my hair. Naomi had told me if I brushed a hundred strokes every day, my hair would be shiny and manageable. I'd been doing it every day for three weeks and I didn't see any difference. Still, it wouldn't hurt to try again.

I counted the brushstrokes in my head — 67, 68 ... I heard a light knock on the bathroom door and said, "Come in."

Mom peeked around the corner. "Do you have a sec, kiddo?"

71, 72 ... I couldn't lose track. "Sure, come on in."

She slipped in and sat on the edge of the tub. "I've been thinking."

75, 76 ... Please, please, say yes.

Mom played with the ring she wore on her right hand. "If this means so much to you — I mean, it won't be easy, not for any of us. But if it's that important — then, yes, your grandmother can come for Christmas dinner."

"Eighty-two!" I said. "I mean, great!" I

104

hugged her hard. I pictured the three of us sitting around the kitchen table singing carols, maybe Mom and Grandma getting all teary and hugging each other.

It was going to be a great Christmas.

11

We were all set. Mom called Grandma after lunch, and Grandma accepted the invitation. I'd been singing "Joy to the World" since Mom told me we'd all be celebrating Christmas together.

We were buying groceries, just like we did every Saturday afternoon, except this time we were shopping for three. As usual, Mom's list was organized by aisle. I looked over her shoulder as we hit the produce department. Aisle one: potatoes, celery, cranberries, beets …

"Beets?" I said. "We hate beets!"

Mom laughed. "Grandma likes them. Why not?"

Mom called her "grandma" instead of "your

grandmother." I was so happy I'd eat anything Mom put on my plate. Maybe even beets.

We splurged on cranberries, stuffing ingredients, a turkey — the same things we bought every Christmas, but this year they would taste better than ever.

After we finished, Mom and I each took a bundle buggy and walked toward the doors. They're supposed to be automatic, but they only opened halfway. I wanted to charge them with my buggy, but Mom shook her head. She turned around and backed into the door, then held it open for me.

The wind smacked my face as I walked out of No Frills. My hat was pulled over my ears as low as it would go. I wrapped my scarf around my face and tucked it in the open spots around my neck. I was even glad to be wearing gloves.

"This is way too cold for December," said Mom. "What's January going to be like?"

As we crossed the street, I saw Prince Charlie standing at his usual corner. His breath made little frozen puffs of air above his head. His hands were stuffed in his pockets, and the Blue Jays cap lay at his feet. When we got closer, I stopped and looked in the cap. About two or three dollars in coins.

Mom was walking behind me, so she had to stop too.

"Harley, what are you doing? Let's go home."

I couldn't walk by Charlie today without doing something. I'd been thinking about him since last week, especially after talking to the homeless guy downtown. But I didn't have enough money to make a difference. I wanted to do something more than toss a handful of change in his cap and walk away.

Charlie shifted his weight from one leg to the other and back again. I was cold — he must be freezing.

I took off my gloves and handed them to him.

Charlie was startled. He took the gloves and held them for a minute, first in one hand, then in both. He gazed at them as if he'd never seen anything more beautiful, squeezing them and pressing them against his face. Finally, he put them on. They were too small and gapped at his wrists. But at least his hands fit in.

He looked me in the eyes and nodded. "Thank you," he said.

"You're welcome." I smiled. "Merry Christmas." I slowly pushed my buggy down the street. My hands were freezing, but my heart felt warm.

"Oh, Harley," said Mom.

It was a good pair of gloves. We couldn't afford another pair like them. But I didn't think that's why her eyes were full of tears.

12

Mom checked her watch again. I looked at the clock on the wall — five-forty.

"Your grandmother is never late," said Mom. Uh-oh. She was calling her "your grandmother" again. That wasn't good.

"Maybe the traffic's bad."

"On Christmas day? I don't get it. She said she'd be here at four-thirty." Mom shook her head. "The turkey's ready to come out. The potatoes will be done at six." She went in the living room and peered out the front window, as if Grandma might be standing in the driveway, waiting for us to call her in.

It had been a good day so far. Mom loved the

gardening gloves I gave her. And how had she known to buy me an outfit from American Eagle? I was dying to ask where she'd hidden my presents, but I'd probably never know. I wasn't going to let on that I had been snooping.

The biggest surprise was the parcel wrapped in brown paper, postmarked from Windsor. Only one person I knew lived in Windsor. I had opened the gift to find a CD player from Frank. "He sent it the day after he visited," Mom had said. I couldn't wait to tell Naomi. Mom didn't say "I told you so," but maybe she was right. Maybe Frank wasn't such a bad guy after all.

But now we were waiting for Grandma. I squirmed in my chair. "I think we should call her. She might have fallen asleep, or lost track of the time."

"Good idea."

I thought she would ask me to call, but she picked up the phone herself. She dialled, then waited and listened. Finally she hung up. "I don't get it."

"She might be on her way here."

Mom picked up oven mitts and opened the oven door. She pulled her head back as the heat hit her face and she slid the turkey out. "Maybe. But she always arrives on time, and she was due here over an hour ago." She turned off the oven.

The turkey was golden brown and plump. My mouth watered as I imagined eating it with fluffy mashed potatoes and gravy. "When Grandma gets here, we're going to have an amazing meal," I said.

The phone rang. Mom and I looked at each other, then she hurried to answer it.

"Hello? Yes — "

Mom twisted the loose handle on the mug cupboard. She said, "Yes" one more time and bit her lower lip.

"Oh, no." She leaned hard against the counter. "Is she all right?"

"What?" I whispered.

Mom waved me off. "Uh-huh, just a minute." She covered the receiver with her hand. "Get me a pen. Quick."

I grabbed a pen from the drawer beside the

fridge. Mom scribbled some notes on the back of the water bill. I tried to read them but couldn't see over her shoulder.

"Thanks. We'll be right there."

She hung up the phone and ran her hands over her face, almost as if she was washing it.

"What's wrong?" I said.

Mom's face was all blotchy and her eyes were bloodshot. "Grandma's been in a car accident." She sounded like she had a frog in her throat.

I felt dizzy. I sat on the floor and rested my head against the cupboard. I heard Mom phoning for a cab, and her voice sounded a hundred miles away. I couldn't remember the last time we had taken a cab somewhere.

After Mom hung up, she bent down and held my hands. "I didn't mean to scare you. But we've got to go the hospital to see her." Mom stood up and looked around the kitchen. "Sorry, Harley, we have to take a pass on Christmas dinner. "

She folded the water bill with the information on it and slipped it in her purse. I rose slowly, like I was on a swaying ship and wasn't sure of my balance. All I knew was this — if I hadn't insisted on having Christmas dinner together, Grandma would be fine.

When the cab arrived, we grabbed our coats and rushed out the door. For the first time since October, I left the house without Mom telling me to zip up my coat. She was in such a hurry, I probably could have walked out without my shoes.

As we pulled out of the driveway, I glanced at the Simpsons' house. I saw a group of happy people through their living-room window.

I watched the beautiful Christmas lights on the houses as we drove down the street. I knew that in every house a family was watching someone at the head of the table carve a turkey. That's what every other family did, every year. I wanted to do that one year. Was that too much to ask?

And I couldn't bear the idea of Grandma being in pain. What if she was hurt badly? I blinked my eyes fast. I pressed my fingernails into my palms. The Christmas lights faded into a blur of tears.

Mom noticed me wiping my eyes with the

back of my hand. "You really love her," she said. She handed me a tissue from her purse and put her arm around my shoulder. "I know you're worried. I am too. We'll be there soon."

Why couldn't I do anything right? This was the worst Christmas ever, and it was all my fault. Why hadn't I let Grandma have a safe, lonely Christmas at home?

When we got to the hospital, the driver pulled up in front of the Emergency entrance. Mom carefully counted out the money to pay him, then followed me out of the cab.

As we went into the Emergency department, I squinted from the bright overhead lights. A tree with some dull balls hanging off the branches stood in the corner of the room. Pine needles were scattered around the base. A nurse bustled by wearing a Santa Claus pin on her uniform.

I leaned against a pillar while Mom went to ask about Grandma. It was warm in here, the kind of heat that made you want to lay your head down and fall asleep.

The Christmas tree was too depressing, so I

turned toward the waiting area. The TV was on, showing a Christmas parade from somewhere warm. A marching band played "Frosty the Snowman" while the majorettes beamed and tossed their batons. A man and a little kid sat in front of the TV. The kid was singing with the band. The only other person in the waiting room was a woman wearing pink track pants sitting in the corner, reading the Bible.

I wished I was watching "White Christmas" at home just as we did every year. Thank goodness we were going to Naomi's house for brunch tomorrow, because today was a disaster.

Mom came back from the nursing station and hugged me. "We can see her in a couple of minutes."

We sat in green vinyl chairs in the middle of the room. I didn't want to watch the parade, but there was nothing else to do. Mickey Mouse was riding on a giant toboggan. He grinned and waved at the crowd. I couldn't stop worrying about Grandma.

Mom took my hand. "What a day! I'm sorry

about the way everything turned out. You tried so hard to get two stubborn women together. You deserve better than this."

I shrugged. "I wish I never invited her."

"You were following your heart. Maybe we can have her over on New Year's instead."

"I bet she's hungry now."

Mom glanced at the vending machines. "Nothing but candy. Let's see if we can find a sandwich somewhere."

"How about a couple of sandwiches?" I said. "I'm hungry, too."

"There's a cafeteria down the hall. If it's open, we'll buy dinner for three."

When we returned, carrying the paper bag with our food, Mom went back to talk to the nurse. After a minute she motioned to me and the nurse led us to Grandma's room. "She'll be better in no time," said the nurse.

Grandma was sitting up in the hospital bed, and she had two black eyes. She seemed happy to see us, but said, "I told them not to bother you."

"Did you think we'd eat Christmas dinner

without you?" Mom asked.

After everything that had happened, I wasn't going to listen to them argue. "No," I said. "No, you're not fighting today." Mom and Grandma stared at me as if they hadn't heard me speak before.

"You're not fighting, because today is Christmas. We said we'd have dinner together, and we will." I placed the paper bag on the bedside table and sat beside Grandma. "We have turkey sandwiches with carrot sticks, and jello with whipped cream for dessert."

Mom and Grandma looked at each other. "Some Christmas dinner, isn't it?" Mom said.

"I'm sorry I missed your meal, Robin," said Grandma. "You were always a better cook than me."

Mom laughed softly. "Remember the year you made gravy with icing sugar instead of flour?"

"It wasn't much worse than my regular gravy."

Another story I hadn't heard. I was dying to hear it, but something more important was going on.

Mom reached across and put her hand next to Grandma on the bed. "The last time we were together in a hospital room, it was Christmas, too," Mom said.

"I was thinking about that before you came. I've never felt the same way about Christmas since then."

"You mean Grandpa?" I asked. He died on Christmas day when I was four.

Grandma turned to me and nodded. "Your mother and I have had our share of arguments, but nobody was kinder to me when your grandpa was dying. He spent the last two weeks of his life in this hospital, and your mother made sure there was always someone here with me."

"It was awful. But you were really strong." Mom swallowed hard. There was silence in the room for a minute. Then Mom patted Grandma's hand. "How are you feeling?" she asked.

"Not bad. I'm a bit shaken up, but otherwise I'm fine. I'm afraid your Christmas presents are still in the car. I would have liked to give them to you tonight."

"Don't worry," said Mom.

"Actually, the main gift I'm giving you, Robin, isn't something that can be wrapped. Harley told me you're going back to school next year. If you'll accept, I'd like to do something to help out. I could pick up Harley after school every day, let her do homework at my place, and bring her home when it's convenient for you."

I gasped. "Oh, Grandma, that would be amazing! Please, Mom?"

Mom's face was flushed as she turned to Grandma. "I don't know what to say. Are you sure you wouldn't mind?"

"I'd love to do it."

Mom waited a moment before speaking. "Sounds like you've got Harley onside, which is more than I've been able to do. I'm still working out the course details, but, yeah, that would help out a lot. Thank you."

I could have sworn Grandma's eyes were watering. She patted my leg and said, "Your gift is already at your house. I gave it to your mother last weekend, before I changed my plans for

Christmas day. I hope you like it." How did she say that with a straight face? She winked at me so Mom wouldn't see.

"Thank you, Grandma."

"I do have another small gift for you in my car. I understand you need a new pair of gloves."

"How did you know?"

"Your mother is very proud of you."

I turned to Mom. "You called Grandma to tell her about Prince Charlie?"

"I called her to check what time she was coming. I guess I mentioned him in passing."

Grandma snorted. "You knew what time I was coming. You called to tell me about Prince Charlie."

So maybe the idea of getting them together wasn't stupid, after all!

Grandma continued. "Harley, when your mother was about your age I gave her a beautiful ankle-length winter coat. The next day, she gave it to one of her classmates who didn't have a coat. Do you remember that, Robin? You wore your old ski jacket all winter without complaining."

"I remember."

"I think you've raised a daughter in your own image."

This was perfect! Then Grandma said, "You know, I'd be happy to pay your tuition, too."

Mom stiffened. "I can pay for it myself."

"Don't be mulish. I'm only trying to help you. It would be so much easier."

Adults! "You're like two peas in a pod," I said. "This is going to work for all of us. Grandma and I will see each other a lot more. And Mom gets to go back to school without a major battle from me. So stop fighting!"

Silence. Then Mom smiled. And Grandma smiled.

"What makes me think this isn't the last lecture we'll get?" Mom asked. She leaned over and hugged me. "Don't ever let us give up on each other. Okay, Harley?"

I nodded.

The sound of "Jingle Bell Rock" wafted in from the waiting room. Our turkey sandwiches were curling up at the corners, and the jello looked like we might need a chainsaw to cut it.

Grandma was right. Mom was a great cook.

But this was the best Christmas dinner ever.